About Leaf Books

Leaf Books' fine and upstanding mission is to support the publication of high quality short fiction, micro-fiction and poetry by both new and established writers.

We have put over 200 authors and poets into print since our inception in 2006. Many of them have never been published before.

See our website at www.leafbooks.co.uk for news, more information about our authors, other titles and having your own work published by Leaf.

Other Leaf Books Anthologies

Available Now:

Coming Soon:

Derek

& More Micro-Fiction

First published by Leaf Books Ltd in 2007

Copyright © The Authors

www.leafbooks.co.uk

Leaf Books Ltd.
GTi Suite,
Valleys Innovation Centre,
Navigation Park,
Abercynon,
CF45 4SN

Printed by Jem
www.jem.co.uk

ISBN-10: 1-905599-36-6
ISBN-13: 978-1-905599-36-3

Contents

Introduction

Leaf Books ran its first Micro-Fiction Competition back in 2006. We were a bit quirkier in those days and we called it the Leaf Books Short Short Story Competition. At that time, we admitted – quite out loud – that judging such a competition was a new experience for us and we didn't quite know what to expect. Now, in our maturity and with two collections of micro-fiction under our collective belts, we feel, essentially, like world-class experts. We've even half a notion that we're the leading publishers for the production of micro-fiction in a printed format, though we're not actually doing any research or giving you any statistics to back up that bit of speculation. We probably are though.

The judging, then, was less of a minefield this time around: while finding the cream's never much of a problem, as essentially it means waiting for it to smack you unrelentingly in the face with its brilliance (I think that's how the analogy goes), we now felt that we knew for sure what we definitely *weren't* looking for and that made the whittling-down stage rather more efficient. In the introduction to *The Final Theory and Other Short Short Stories*, we identified one major failing to which those attempting but not quite succeeding to get their heads around this trickiest of formats tended to fall prey: twist-in-the-tale endings that seem a tempting means of injecting a bit of interest into an otherwise prosaic piece of work and generally do nothing more than undermine the preceding narrative before falling depressingly flat. We're thankful to report that, to our endless pleasure, there was significantly less of that sort of thing rearing its head in the 2007 competition. But there was a new most-popular wrong turning that we hadn't been expecting… an area where a significant number of the stories went slightly astray. Many of the entrants, quite simply, wrote too much. Not too much for the stipulated word limit or anything: just too much for the stories they were writing. This may be symptomatic of our having raised the upper word limit from 300 to 500 – a number of entrants did seem keen to get value for their entry fees – but this competition undeniably lacked the proliferation of wonderfully concise, epigrammatic little two-sentence and single paragraph stories that were, by and large, our favourite pieces in the previous comp. The vast majority of the 2007 entries really pushed the 500-word mark, and too often it turned out to be either more or less wordage than those stories truly had in them: they were truncated short stories, which is less ideal, or nice little single paragraph pieces with 200 words of padding. We hope this observation shan't massively upset those who wrote 497-word stories and failed to make it into the anthology, but it was such a striking issue that we thought it worth mentioning for future reference.

That said, we did nonetheless find no fewer than thirty-seven face-smackingly brilliant stories that we felt more than worthy of inclusion in this anthology: fluently written pieces that, vitally, are stories in and of themselves rather than isolated observations; that don't rely on insufficiently foreshadowed twists and that don't take up an inch more space on the page than is strictly necessary. It's as varied a bundle as ever. There's a tale of a visit to an alien planet during which the intruders lack the imagination to even recognise the story's protagonists as sentient beings in the shape of 'Callers' by the prolific Sue Anderson: it reminded the team powerfully of the sort of unintentionally deadly well-meaningness that Captain Kirk used to bring down on alien species on a weekly basis in the late sixties, and that made us wistful and nostalgic. One of the most imaginative stories in the collection is Don Taylor's 'Mountain Air Footie', in which various cultural differences are bridged by pure, glorious silliness when Western tourists, Kyrgyz truckers and Chinese soldiers unite over a game of imaginary football. And there are serious pieces as well as the comic: Laurie Porter's wrenching 'We'll Meet Again' about a man's ostensibly macabre but oddly touching plan to be reunited once again with the wife he left decades ago, for example, and Amy Sackville's 'Signalling', a poignant portrait of a failing relationship that manages to convey exactly the hideous tension in the car full of alienated family members without every overtly stating what precisely is going on.

There were ultimately two or three stories vying for the coveted top spot. 'You are my giraffe now' by Jason Jackson was certainly a prime contender: a first-person narration to a stuffed giraffe was obviously going to push most of our buttons from the off, but the superbly-realised voice of the obviously disturbed, possibly institutionalised and touchingly optimistic speaker takes it beyond the quirky and into the distinctly significant. Another highly-rated story was 'Picture Your Father Without A Picture' by Teresa Stenson: an extended simile that's a mixture of brilliantly observed comic dialogue (a child envisions her absent father as 'like a potato' after her mother describes him as 'Solid. Of the earth. Earthy.') and genuine, underplayed angst.

But the prize went, in the end, to Gina Goodwin (who has two pieces in the collection) for her entirely charming and faintly unsettling story 'Derek', in which the eponymous main character vexes his long-suffering wife by (apparently) astral-projecting all over the garden in a state of semi-undress. The telling is just beautifully straightforward and economic, pared down to the absolute minimum, and seething with peculiarly British details about Sweetheart cabbages and y-fronts that lend it a sort of divine comic mundanity. It's never made clear if we're witnessing a genuine but wonderfully surreal bit of a fantasy or if something's amiss in Derek's mind, all of which makes for a very open and rewarding piece of writing to which the reader can most fruitfully return. And we said in our summing up of the previous competition that the winning story would suggest a novel's worth of telling in its couple of hundred or so words. 'Derek' suggests two entire lives.

Our thanks to all who entered.

The Stories

Gina Goodwin

After selling her business, Gina Goodwin moved to a ruin in West Wales where she has now lived for nearly two years; almost as long as she's lived anywhere. When the weather is fine, she can be found helping with the renovations or trying to create a garden from the wilderness. She shares this life with her partner, Jack Russell puppy and their four cats. Having been writing since her teens, Gina starts new projects with enthusiasm; unfortunately, up until now, life has seemed to interfere to stop her from actually finishing anything. She has two grown up sons and three grandchildren.

Derek

Susan was walking back into the vegetable garden with a mug of tea she'd fetched from the house, and almost dropped it in surprise. She put the cup down on the table under the large apple tree and stared at Derek, who was wandering around in the rhubarb patch in nothing but black socks, slippers and a pair of y-fronts. He was rubbing his chin, thoughtfully.

Susan asked him what he was doing there. He didn't seem to know. But when he explained that he'd been lying on the bed reading a book on astral travel only five minutes before, it all became very clear – to him, at least.

'I must have travelled through time,' he said, looking very relieved. He glanced at his watch. It had moved on since the last time he checked, but he couldn't remember by how much. 'Never mind. At least I'm here,' he mumbled to himself.

Susan asked him where he'd left his trousers, but he wasn't sure. Although he thought he remembered leaving his shirt in the cabbage patch.

She went to look and sure enough there was something there. She moved closer. A pair of trousers lay across two rows of Sweethearts, the early variety. She retrieved them and walked towards the runner beans where she found his shirt.

By the time she arrived back at the rhubarb patch, Derek had left. His y-fronts, however, had stayed. She gathered them up and followed the trail.

A slipper; she retrieved it. Another slipper, then two socks and finally Derek. He was sitting on the bench, legs crossed, drinking her tea.

Jason Jackson

Jason Jackson lives in Bristol with his wife and son. His short stories have appeared online and in print, including the recent Leaf collection *The Final Theory and Other Stories.*

You are my giraffe now

You are my giraffe now, and I will converse with you. You will listen, although to have cloth ears is an issue we will have to deal with. It is strange, to speak to a giraffe, but it must be even stranger to be a giraffe. A cloth, stuffed giraffe.

So we are both strange. That is good.

I have been here too long, and your presence will do little to change the situation. But perhaps you will relieve me of burdensome feelings. It is a hard life, to only talk to giraffes, or elephants, or an occasional teddy bear. Not Disney characters. I will not have them near me. It is their fur. Too soft. And their eyes know things I would prefer they didn't.

But you, my cloth giraffe, are perfect. I'm sorry young Steven is no longer here to be your friend. He recommended your conversation. You are, he said, a nice giraffe.

You see out there? The lake? It is my goal. And you can help. Oh, what it would be to reach that lake! But it is so far! Too far for me. Or, at least, it has always seemed that way. But perhaps with you? Perhaps with a silent, cloth-eared giraffe, the lake will become reachable. To stand there in the rain, and even throw a stone! It would be good, would it not?

I am sick to the stomach of the stale air in this place.

Your expression puzzles me. It seems full of hope, yet those glassy eyes suggest nothing more than boredom. I do not wish to bore you. Perhaps we should think of the lake again?

I would carry you, of course, under my smock. It is wet outside, and rain does not mix with a cloth giraffe. This is one thing I know. But the rain will be nice. It will make little bumps on my arm, a thing I have not had for too long. And a wet face, a wet neck, wet soles of my feet. These are things to aim for.

And to be under the water for a while! Steven told me he swam there, once. Not for long. The nurses stopped him. He was scolded, locked up.

He did not take you home, with smiling parents and sweet-smelling sister. No. You, his only giraffe, you are here with me.

We will not go to the lake today. We need to know each other better. But the lake is a goal of mine, as I have said. A goal I will share with you, my giraffe.

I have no one else.

There are other goals too. There is so much for us to aim for! Time may be short, but you are my giraffe now, and everything is possible.

Amy Mackelden

Amy Mackelden studied her MA in Creative Writing at Cardiff Uni. Now, she works in a bookshop and writes lots of little stories about her ex-boyfriends.

Imaginary Origami

We've only ever eaten sushi when we've eaten out together, because Jack thinks we're in *Lost in Translation*. He keeps recreating Japan in the smallest of ways, and I'm acutely aware of this. I almost feel misplaced.

Lately, it's not just sushi and sashimi. Jack's been folding paper into particular patterns and making tempura from scratch. He doesn't listen when I tell him China folded paper first, and that tempura's Portuguese – something about missionaries, and Lent, and battered fish not being meat.

To remind Jack where we're not, I unfold folded sheets of paper and eat all meat cooked but not battered – I get around his preferences. Jack gets around mine. He lets me pick which Bill Murray film we watch. Then he makes paper flowers for me, and says, 'Stop trying to change me, Scarlett Johannson.'

Gina Goodwin

After selling her business, Gina Goodwin moved to a ruin in West Wales where she has now lived for nearly two years; almost as long as she's lived anywhere. When the weather is fine, she can be found helping with the renovations or trying to create a garden from the wilderness. She shares this life with her partner, Jack Russell puppy and their four cats. Having been writing since her teens, Gina starts new projects with enthusiasm; unfortunately, up until now, life has seemed to interfere to stop her from actually finishing anything. She has two grown up sons and three grandchildren.

Badger Play

There's a full moon tonight. The badgers are out at play-disguised-as-work.

Pointed snouts plough the field. Tussocks of disembodied grass, tossed into the air, now lie upside down all around them. White stripes catch the light as they go to work. One, presumably a youngster, jumps as an imaginary human passes by and another, presumably an elder, butts him in the side. He goes back to his work. Worms, caterpillars, bugs of any kind; enough to last the long night's day.

They can't see me. I'm squatting in the bushes. My knees ache and I slide slowly onto my side. A twig snaps. Five pairs of eyes fix on me. I close mine and when I open them again, they're gone.

Jason Jackson

Jason Jackson lives in Bristol with his wife and son. His short stories have appeared online and in print, including the recent Leaf collection *The Final Theory and Other Stories*.

Backwards

Stop the world. Just here.

Good.

Now rewind.

Slowly.

Watch me drifting back from sleep. Watch the girl beside me doing the same.

We're awake again.

Turn the sound down. Can't understand what we're saying when it's running backwards like this.

What?

Okay, a little context. She's angry with me, because it's after midnight and I woke her up. Not my fault. The train was late, then the taxi rank was full of drunken idiots. And she's got work tomorrow.

Wait! There's a bit I'm waiting to see just here – wait – slow it down – there!

Hit pause.

Smiling. She's smiling at me. We might be arguing, but there's a smile there, right?

Yeah. I though so too.

I want to freeze that. Can you print it off?

Great. It's important, for the stuff later on.

Or earlier.

Whatever.

Right. Now we're downstairs, and I'm outside, banging on the door. Into the taxi. You can speed this stuff up if you like. Yeah, and this. It's a long train journey. I read half a novel. Shared my lager with two blokes in the seats opposite. London's a long way from Newcastle.

Speed it up.

More.

Right. When the train stops, slow everything down.

There! Yeah, right down. I want to see this.

There she is. On the platform. She's quite attractive really. What do you think? Better than the other one?

No, you're right. That's not the point.

I'm first off the train. That means I must've been last on. I hadn't realised that.

Right. This is the bit I need to see.

There. She's crying. Freeze it.

I hug her, she pulls back, and she's crying.

Can you print that one too?

Right.

Can I have both printouts?

Because this is what I want to see. I want to see her crying, the girl I'm saying goodbye to, and I want to see the other one smile. But I need to see them both at the same time.

What do you mean, why?

Because I want to see if the one was worth the other. I want to see if the smile was worth the tears.

You can't do it?

No. I suppose you're right. The world doesn't work like that, does it? Be nice though, wouldn't it? Just to see, you know.

Check I did the right thing.

What?

Oh, yeah, you can switch it off now.

Just switch it off.

Amy Mackelden

Amy Mackelden studied her MA in Creative Writing at Cardiff Uni. Now, she works in a bookshop and writes lots of little stories about her ex-boyfriends.

Lee & Holly

You take me seriously after *Hannah and her Sisters*. Before that you get surprised I'm twenty-three (although you *did* know – I guess you just forgot), and you didn't know about church, and knowing that makes me disownable. Well, not really: it just catches you, so that I'm not completely who you thought I was.

I don't know who you thought I was. We've been fighting for fifteen days now, possibly more, and we don't run out of material – there are always more ways to make fun of Nietzsche, and micro-fiction, or that fact that I'm published, but not really.

You're inept, and I'm incompetent, and it's all kind of cute, although it shouldn't be. I don't make it into more than it is, because I'm scared to do that. I haven't asked about girlfriends, or boyfriends, even. What I know is select, and it's only now we're alone that I get specifics – like the title of your thesis, and what it is you might do later – not tonight, but next year. It's almost next year now, so I think it's okay asking. I've not got resolutions, and I won't ask you to give up anything. You're all right, I think.

You light one smoke inside, and one once we're out. You leave while it's still early, and tomorrow say you shouldn't have. You say it flippantly and it falls between insults. It's lodged, anyway.

Amy Mackelden

Amy Mackelden studied her MA in Creative Writing at Cardiff Uni. Now, she works in a bookshop and writes lots of little stories about her ex-boyfriends.

Heavy Petting

He got on two stops from her house, ignored empty seats, said, 'I'll give you a rest today,' to the girl in front, then sat next to Katie. His leg touched hers as he sat down and she sensed thighs spreading inside grey polyester trousers.

This man smells like dogs and cough sweets. Katie's stomach is unsettled even after cereal, and when she breathes, she swears stray white dog hairs end up in her lungs. This mixed with the honey-lemon cocktail – the smell hits Katie before it hits the window – makes bran flakes congeal, and Katie's fingers feel sticky.

Boys at the back of the bus spray aerosols under their shirts because they forgot somewhere between breakfast and text books, but it doesn't work like adverts. There aren't flocks of girls: just a couple, giggling, more bored than anything, with minutes to kill before they're at school talking to boys who've tried shaving. Nothing works, not even spray, until you're twenty-five, or six, or seven, and even then it's slim pickings.

The cheap-suited man in Katie's seat keeps dogs in a small house, and each morning he lowers one foot to the ground, feeling for newly-malted insulation, grey and white hair covering the space between floorboards and his feet. It's smoother than socks or carpet, but it's starting to stick to him, which could be considered a downside.

Katie's breathing, and the dog hair is sticking to her lung walls, held in place with lozenge, which solidifies once it's inside her, after being inside him. Katie starts wheezing, fumbles for her inhaler, and wonders whether the man even has dogs. Maybe this is just how polyester smells before nine in the morning. Tomorrow, she's walking.

Catherine Edmunds

Catherine Edmunds is an author, musician and artist whose first novel, *The Sand in the Painting*, was published in 2005. Since then, her poetry and short stories have appeared in numerous online and print journals and anthologies published by Leaf Books, Earlyworks Press, Pemmican Press, *14* magazine and others. Recent competition successes include a couple of wins in the *Guardian*'s topical haiku contest, a Highly Commended poem in the Plough Prize, and Highly Commended flash fiction in the last two Twisted Tongue competitions. Catherine is also an illustrator who has provided the artwork for three book covers for Earlyworks Press.

The Crumb

'It's just a bread roll,' she laughs, confused, but this is no French stick from a Peckham deli – it's a baguette, the real thing, bought not five minutes ago from a Paris boulangerie.

'No, listen, love: there's a sweetness, or, no, not a sweetness exactly…' My thoughts wander as I take another bite, the crust lightly grazing my gums as my teeth sink through to the moist centre and camembert spreads its silken cream through my mouth like a benediction.

'Itsh efquiffith,' I tell her.

'You what?' she splutters.

I have to share this experience. Have to show her.

'You're in Paris, woman! Here. Try. Taste.'

She shrugs. It's a very Gallic gesture and unexpectedly appropriate. I break off a piece, scattering crumbs over the boulevard in the process, and hand it to her. She nibbles, then looks up thoughtfully to meet my eyes. There is a stray crumb on her upper lip. I choose not to tell her, as I like the way passers-by are drawn by the sight.

'It's okay, I suppose,' she says, licking her lips but just missing the flake of crust that has impaled itself oh so gently just beyond reach of her tongue.

'Okay? Is that all you can say? Are you mad?'

I'm definitely not telling her about the crumb.

I catch hold of her hand and we turn our backs on the Seine to walk up the Rue de Bièvre, glimpsing the Panthéon through the afternoon gloom. She hops and skips, trying to keep up with my stride, but I don't feel inclined to slow down.

'What's that then?' she asks, pointing to one of the glories of Paris.

'Do you know nothing?'

She shrugs again.

I sigh. A knowledge of Paris is not a prerequisite for love, after all. Or is it?

'It's the Panthéon, darling.'

'Panthéon? Is that like a zoo? Where they keep panthers?'

'No, you silly woman – ' I stop. She's laughing at me.

'Joke, sweetie,' she winks. 'Woohoo – yummy!'

I'm embarrassed. People stop and stare at this untidy woman with her raucous exclamations who peers through the window of a brasserie, nearly toppling all six foot four of me over by tugging on my arm. The place is filled with Parisians – so chic and elegant – who consume their food with an air that is utterly alien to her. And to me too, if I'm honest. I feel enormous. Why are Parisians so tiny? My feet are too big. I am monstrous. I apologise silently to my beloved city, and murmur, 'I think I need Champagne'.

'Asti's just not the same, is it, ducks,' she chuckles, knowing my moods so well.

I smile at this fair flower of Peckham Rye, who leans on my arm and blooms so brightly on a grey October afternoon in Paris.

'There's a crumb,' I tell her.

'A crumb?'

'On your upper lip. Here, let me....'

Not a Good Idea

If you lift the lid of the cold frame, the rotten wood will fall apart and the glass will fall and break and pierce the soil, and maybe, just maybe, strike the corpse underneath, because I didn't bury it very deep (the ground being frozen) so I wouldn't do that if I were you. No, really. Trust me.

Sara Benham

Sara Benham lives in the Westcountry with her partner and two children. She writes as a community correspondent for a local newspaper, and also works part time as an estate agent. Sara began writing short stories and comedy sketches after attending a year-long creative writing course at her local college. Humour plays a big part in Sara's writing and in her life: she also writes and performs stand up comedy.

The Truth About Janet

Mother led me by the hand through to the kitchen, away from the din of the party.

'Now you've become a grown up, like – being as you've turned eighteen, Pappy and me thought it best to tell you… the truth.'

I leaned back against the fridge, gripping the sides with clammy hands.

Mother looked at me, her eyes wide like a codfish. 'Janet,' she said sternly as she straightened my shirt collar, 'you was adapted.'

I let go of the fridge. 'I was adopted?'

'Nope. Adapted. See, you'm kind of… different.'

'What?'

Mother huffed and elbowed Pappy. 'Tell her, Ron.'

Pappy was rolling some smoking tobacco. He didn't look up. He huffed too.

'You began life as a large slug. We found you on the doorstep in the rain and took you in as our own.'

'But I've got arms and legs, Pappy,' I said, doing a little Night Fever kind of dance.

'Robotic arms and legs. The family had a whip round and we did a couple of car-boots to raise the 7.4 million pounds needed to have they buggers grafted on by the best slug-humanoid surgeon money could buy.'

Pappy was an eloquent man, even though he'd worked packing cellophane all his life. I often wondered what they wrapped the cellophane in, and made a mental note to ask Pappy next time we were on the subject.

He spoke again. 'You must accept that you are probably the only robotic slug living as a human being.'

'Except for John Prescott,' Mother added.

Pappy looked up and rubbed my arm in the same way he did if I didn't win the toy in the Christmas cracker. 'Except for John Prescott, obviously.'

'Still,' said mother, turning to the sink to start the washing up. 'At least it explains your poor figure and that excessive trail of mucus you've lived with all your life.'

I stared at the back of her head. She mumbled something about wishing she had the same excuse and took her best soft dishcloth from under the sink, so as not to rub the orange flowers off her favourite white glass teacups.

I could hear Granny playing 'Froggy Went a Courtin' on the Spanish guitar in the next room and edged towards the door, desperate to get back to normality.

'Best we don't speak of this again, Janet. We just thought you should know.'

Pappy smiled and poked his lower set of false teeth so far out they were almost lost to the grimy lino below. He always did this to make me laugh. I smiled back, opened the living room door, and shut it quickly behind me.

Rusty looked up from playing with the whippet. 'Hey, Jan, what did they tell you this year? Abducted by aliens? Half-human, half-vegetable?'

'Something like that,' I said and turned to join Granny in a sing-a-long.

'Froggy went a courtin' and he did ride, a sword and a pistol by his side, hmm… '

Teresa Stenson

Teresa Stenson serves latte to pay the bills and daydreams of the Booker Prize as she froths milk. Her short stories have been published in several anthologies, including *With Islands In Mind* from Earlyworks Press and *The Dreaming Paintbrush* collection. She is currently making a short film based on one of her stories with hum-drum Films. She is at her happiest with a cinnamon whirl in one hand and a cup of good coffee in the other.

Picture Your Father Without A Picture

What is he like? – that's the question Sylvie needed an answer to.

'He's nice.'

'Think of a better word.'

'He's good.'

She stared at her mother who, instead of staring back, shook her head and twirled her hands and fingers in the air as she said, 'Solid. Of the earth. Earthy.'

'Like a potato?'

'Mmmm.'

And so for years she knew he:

grew in fields and

was kept under the sink

or in other dark, cool places of their tiny house.

Have you even got a Dad? – that was the question the kids at school wanted an answer to.

She asked her mother, 'Is he really like a potato?'

Her mother waved an arm out and circled her hand in the air. 'Yes.'

And so for a few more years he:

was roasted

though mainly baked

and sometimes fried.

Until it wasn't enough for her anymore. Sylvie followed her mother around the house, through doors, into rooms and out again until eventually she turned to face her, arms crossed. 'Don't look at me like that. Why are you looking at me like that?'

'What kind of potato?'

Her mother sighed. 'I don't know. I just said it. We were having chips for tea.'

'Is he a chip?'

'No. He's… a potato before. Before all of that. He is good, solid, of the earth.'

And then one day Sylvie stood at the raw potato's door. When he answered he was tall, stooped and drained.

'Like a French fry that's too long. The one you pick up and hold up and show to your friends and say "look at how long this is".' These were her first, disappointed words to her Father.

'But it's been a long time,' were his to her.

Su Barkla

Su Barkla has been writing all her life and is a member of Exeter Writers. She is at present working on a young adults' fantasy series of four novels. 'The Tower' is her first piece of micro-fiction and is the result of a lifelong devotion to MR James's ghost stories.

The Tower

Halfway up the hill stands the folly: a tower with high, narrow, glazed windows and a weathercock. The door is heavy, of cross-grained panels, solidly locked. No-one is ever seen to go inside.

This is because it belongs to the cousins, John and Richard, who are away at the wars. It was a favourite place of theirs from childhood.

Inside the tower it is quiet and empty. There is a circle of stone-flagged floor and a wooden table with a lantern on it.

You would not notice after dark that one of the flagstones is uneven, from the night when Richard could not set it straight. You would not know that under the flagstones is a small but strong locked chest, and that under the chest is John's body. But after all, thinks Richard, the stone will remind him where the money is.

It is after dark that Richard will come back, after waiting a little while down in the town – for everyone to rejoice over his return, and to mourn the death of John overseas.

And it is there in the tower that John is waiting for him.

Cath Drake

Cath Drake has earned most of her living from writing and communications. She specialised in environmental issues in her native Australia for almost a decade where she won awards for her writing and radio programmes. She has written everything from nature trails, to radio programmes, newspaper and magazine articles, pamphlets and books. Cath moved to London in 2001 and now works part-time in a children's charity in PR, runs creative writing workshops and writes poetry and short stories. She is part of a performance poetry collective, Malika's Kitchen, whose anthology *A Storm Between Fingers* has just been published.

Going Home

'I don't want to go home. It just occurred to me today. I hadn't thought about it before. I have been here for four days and I don't want to go home. I now know what it's been like every day for the last twenty six years.'

Susan cannot believe what she is hearing. She would rather not hear it. She does her best to ignore it; it makes her nervous. She arranges the flowers she brought in the vase at the end of Fran's bed. She had only just arrived, followed the bedded corridors and florescent hospital signs, and said hello. That was all she'd said so far and Fran hadn't even said hello in return.

Susan arranges the flowers for much longer than she needs to, exacting the spaces between them and concentrating on their perfume.

'The lilies smell so sweet. I just picked them today,' she says, as she looks at Fran, hoping she would take her words back and talk about something else – anything else. She is afraid, more afraid than Fran at this moment.

'I don't want to go home,' Fran says again, just has clearly as last time.

They stare at each other while Susan hopes Fran will talk about the flowers or the weather or the hospital food. But she doesn't. She says nothing. Nothing to add. Susan looks around her at the nearby beds, white walls, clean towels hanging on steel racks. Fran's feet are poking through starched white sheets. There's a half-eaten lunch on the bedside table, a cluster of pastel-coloured cards, tissues, vases, some drooping daisies.

'You don't really mean that. You can't stay here,' Susan says.

Fran cannot answer.

'Some nice cards you've got.'

Fran does not look at the cards. 'He nags. He nags and he nags, and I won't go home,' she says.

Susan is desperate that this conversation should stop. She has no line to take.

'Where else could you go? You have to go home,' she says.

She arranges the flowers again, chats to a passing nurse, tells them both about her trouble parking and the misleading traffic light on the way in. Fran's tea arrives. Susan helps her pour the milk, asks her if she has enough, wants another cushion, another biscuit, anything else?

'Can I get you anything from home? Do you need extra nighties? Underpants? Hand cream?'

Fran hardly replies. She faintly acknowledges the questions with her eyes. What does she need? But soon the visit is over and the next time Susan comes they talk of flowers and hospital food and traffic lights. Susan watches Fran arrange her cards on the bedside table.

Jo Else

Jo Else is a slacker/receptionist whose jobs have varied from using hairdryers to drying out money found in the Thames to making up fiction for new Labour Party politicians (i.e. writing their speeches). A career, albeit obscure, in the literary arts was inevitable. Jo lives in an insalubrious part of London with her cat Fisher, her guinea pig Titian, and her partner, a piano teacher and performer. She has recently completed a poetry anthology, *A Border Collie Sings The Blues*, and a number of flash fiction pieces, and is also a performance poet on the London poetry circuit.

And I'm Gone

Clutching the strap, hoping for an end to the endless going on; the perpetuation of all things dreary. Collapsing next to a woman. Praying that the black material covering everything but her eyes conceals a large explosive device. At the point of extinction to reintegrate, not disintegrate, his spirit finally alive, free from death-life; job, wife… especially wife. *Candice, you prison wall: no going round you, though you, over you.*

'So you want out,' the old man whispers. To his left: white hair, beige summer suit, holding Jamie's eye, casually pulling back his jacket to reveal a neat line of grenades round his waist. 'Packs a good punch,' he laughs. *Hoax, must be…* but Jamie's clobbering, thumping heart disagrees. He sees screaming bodies toppling over each other, severed limbs, annihilation in darkness. How rats die. *Believed I was ready. I'm not.* The irritating survival instinct kicking in, frustrating his greater purpose.

'Relax.' His thoughts read. 'Why so afraid?' says the old man. 'Given what you were just thinking.'

Keep the old idiot talking… but panic glues Jamie's tongue to the top of his mouth.

'You're wondering why, Jamie. Well, nothing gives me joy, and as for this lot… ' – gesturing with veined flexible hands around him – '… too busy protecting themselves to live. Can't care for them. But you mistake yourself. You crave life, not death. I'll detonate at Finsbury Park. Leave at Seven Sisters: get far away. Self-sacrifice is always vile.'

James moves rapidly towards the exit. The old man could change his mind – *he's crazy: any second he'll…* Jamie sprints along the platform, up the down escalator, people swearing, screaming at him. Fast into a black cab to Walthamstow, expecting muffled explosions, sirens any minute. Nothing.

Two hours persuading the bank to release half his mother's house sale money; back home for his passport; gone.

2pm. Stansted express, en route to an evening flight. Remembering Candice, he's furious suddenly: the fertility tests, her smirk at the clinic; assuming the problem was his. *Not your property, Candice, to be tested, prodded. You forgot my rights. The right to avoid compulsory parenthood, the right to love, befriend where I choose, the right not to answer to you.* Love, once a police state, ceases to be love. She'd never understand; he'd not try to make her.

Touch down, Malaga, checking the terminal TV screens. Bombs in Baghdad, Basra; business as usual. Grim former holiday-makers littering the seats, waiting to be called back to the Grey Isle. *Don't go back*, he almost pleads with them. *But we must*, their eyes say, silently. *We must.* To the cabs, a young Arab driver opening the car door; his lips, silent, full dark, creasing into a welcome, and Jamie's guts sliding, liquefying, expanding. *My soul's change*, he thinks, at last; *my aspect to the sun altering, rising. The old man fooled me and it doesn't matter. It will never matter.* At his mouth's left corner, a smile emerges, spreads over his face like a blemish.

I, Witch

Dead in there and it would be over. Dead at forty-eight, like your father, heart-shattered, creasing over whilst he broke stones. But you breathe; a boy's soft, sleeping, furious face. I want to stroke back the grey black hair troubling your forehead, unhook you from your hurts, but I am bitter. You failed to recognise my worth; failed to see the pieces of bright emerald brushed casually from your shoes like sand. You saw me yet you did not *see* me; sinning by omission, but still sinning.

The things I want to say, always the things I want to say, now whispered viciously to you in deep blank early morning. Watch your closed eyes; remember the skin of your face, icy to my touch from a March evening in our past. In my mind I place my right hand on your cheek; my left lies gently on your chest. I thrust my fingers deep into your flesh, sense your heart muscles expand, contract and cover my hand. The dirty, windowless basement room you keep for me inside your head is suddenly clean, sparking; aglow with the light of red candles and jet and malachite and rose quartz and carpets of pearls.

I leave you dreaming and mumbling in your bed while I float down the stairs with flimsy painted chains passing for banisters; once hip, part of the golden Paul and Jonathan days. He left ten years ago and now they're tatty, sad – plain metal showing through chipped silver paint. I step inside your study; chapel-hushed, thick with old cigar smoke and everywhere books; books lining cases, stacked up on tables, floors, cupboards, chairs. Screensavers flicker from your two computer; blue diamonds dance into squares and tetrahedrons, rhomboids, back into squares again. White lilies, unfresh, still fragrant, drop from a glass vase to the floor as, outside, wood pigeons crush their wings against the trees, and I can sense you here so clearly. They fail you yet in this room you can remake yourself; use words to bind up wounds.

Finished, I make myself into a narrow beam of light passing through your roof, then gliding over railway lines, motorways, farms, and ancient hedgerows, crossing water; the water back to London. River, lakes, garden ponds, and streams and reservoirs; reflected in them all, my arms outstretched. Near Rugby a white cat, eyes blood orange, glares up; hares shrug in fields near Crewe. Home. I bolt back, down into my shell again, curl up my legs like a small animal. The phone rings and tracks onto ansaphone. Your voice; sleep – sodden, urgent, afraid. Hearing your fear I know my roots begin to grow in you: dark green, twining, intractable. A love under water, small bubbles rising up from me for twenty years; and now I surface, take in the air, survey my kingdom.

Don Taylor

Don is a former gardener, labourer, assistant librarian, Kibbutz volunteer, trawler hand, hydrometry assistant, drama and art teacher, programmer and senior manager. A great traveller, he actually did play air-football with Chinese border guards, has climbed Mont Blanc and lost his hat to a Kyrgyz horseman. Don lives a quieter life in rural Essex with his wife, dog and MA in Theory of Linguistics certificate. As well as writing, he enjoys beating the hell out of his tennis ball machine.

Mountain Air Footie

Out in the high wilderness between China and Kyrgyzstan lies the Torugart Pass. Look it up – it's legendary. Here, we fought the Chinese. Well, me, my guide and some Kyrgyz truckers.

It was freezing at the customs post. The officials hadn't yet arrived for that obscure period regarded as opening time. We stamped our feet in the small sunlit square before the padlocked doors and snorted steam like winter horses. Out of boredom, I pretended to kick a ball to Ismail, my Uygur guide.

He was a little crazy too. Kicked the damn thing back.

Five young Chinese soldiers manned the post. They stood stiff with cold and delegated authority. I kicked the ball to one of them. After a few seconds of hesitation, he thawed into a grin, and made an embarrassed but really neat return. His comrades pretended to ignore him and stared into the blue distance.

The waiting truckers were tough men, centrally heated with vodka. The close-cabined fug of a thousand miles was on their leather jackets. They blew warm breath into their hands. I kicked the ball to them. No reaction, apart from scanning me with lazy eyes. So I walked intently towards them, as if to reclaim the ball.

Now, I swear this really happened. The biggest trucker stuck out his palm as a stop signal, just like a New York traffic cop. He bent down. And picked up the non-existent ball. Eighteen stone of suspended belief is quite something. It was kind of alpha-male endorsement. He handed this lump of empty space to one of the other Kyrgyz drivers, who examined it. The third even pointed to a few flaws and rubbed at them with a wet thumb.

The Chinese soldiers showed more interest. The most senior wagged his finger like a fast wind-screen wiper. 'No!' he seemed to be saying as he went up to the truckers. He took the ball. And replaced it with a superior piece of Chinese nothingness. He went back to his comrades sniggering.

The big trucker pondered for a while, then put the replacement in the middle of the small square. 'Okay,' he seemed to be saying. 'You're on.' The other truckers, Ismail and I took five-a-side positions behind him. The Chinese soldiers, with military precision, mirrored our formation.

And we played. No lines. No goal posts. Just the rules of imagination. Sure, there were some awkward moments. Disputed tackles meant two balls in play for a while – but superior acting decided the outcome. Offside was a farce.

After twenty minutes, at 3-2 to us, the soldiers suddenly froze to attention. A black 4x4 had turned into the square. Propriety stepped sharply out of the passenger door, his peaked cap mountainous on his small frame. The customs officer. He hadn't seen the game, but it was in any event over.

In the sudden stillness, a mangy rug of a dog had dashed off with the ball.

Stella Pierides

Stella Pierides writes prose and poetry. Her work has been included in the Anthology *Dance the Guns to Silence* (Flipped Eye, 2005), in *Spiked*, *The Quiet Feather*, *Aesthetica*, the online *Muse Apprentice Guild*, and *Big Pond Rumours*. She has co-edited *Even Paranoids Have Enemies* (Routledge, 1998) and *Beyond Madness* (JKP, 2002). Forthcoming poems are to appear in the anthology of the Word for Word Writers Group. She is member of English PEN, Word for Word and Munich Writers.

The Miracle

In September last year, I made a pact with the patron Saint of St George, a small chapel in the outskirts of Athens. We shared a similar problem. The walls of his church were crumbling and he was in need of donations to repair it. The walls of my heart were crumbling – a hole had appeared in between the atria, and I needed his help to close it. The deal was that I would deposit one hundred and fifty Euros in the church restoration bank account. In return, he would heal the hole in my heart.

I made good my promise immediately. I have the payment slip to prove it. I am sorry to say he did not keep his part of the deal. True enough; the cardiologists could no longer see the hole. They thought the previous doctors incompetent and unprofessional to give me the wrong diagnosis. And they grew impatient with my assurances that my heart had been 'holy' for years. I felt they were questioning my sanity and was, naturally, outraged. I thought them patronising, cold and way off the mark and stormed out of the consulting rooms bathed in sweat. 'Think of it as a miracle,' their chief shouted after me. I was too upset to notice.

In January this year, my cheque to the bank was returned. The account, I was told, had been closed. And soon after, on my quarter-yearly check-up to be precise, the hole reappeared. It was there, as large as a well and glaring like the eye of God.

Sue Anderson

Sue Anderson lives in Monmouth. She thinks of herself as a short story writer, but sometimes has an irresistible urge to write poetry. This tendency has recently been encouraged by the emergence of a small poetry group, Poets in Progress, which meets monthly for lots of lively criticism, inspiration, and, most important of all, coffee and biscuits.

Callers

They're so strange, they are. Oh, not to look at: two legs, straight up, faces of a kind. We're used to that. But to feel – the soft, gluey texture of them on your nerve ends (worse when they get excited); and to hear – all that busy chirping, vibrating the air, trying to get through. Smell I won't go into, and they object to being digested, apparently, so no data on taste.

Psy? Well that's the most important, isn't it? So how do they psy? That's the strangest bit of all.

I was there when they came in. We knew they were landing and we gathered for the reception. Mamod was going to give the speech, you know, and hand over the keys. He had the rock blossoms ready.

The thing started badly because we didn't know if the vehicle was a mother or an artefact: lots of chirping inside and it split open mother-fashion. But when they were all out, we realised that it was definitely some kind of less-alive with extensions.

So now these travellers rushed towards us, very quick, and the psy was terrible. Lots of sparks – good/bad, love/hate, fear/aggression, going on and on all the time quick-quick and you couldn't catch on to anything. Most of the other visitors we've had found a way to contact us. Oh, some of it wasn't nice, but at least you got a definite colour. Argu, for example, they were purple – sad with touches of hope. Kayo were quite lurid. They wanted to kill us all, but it turned out all right, in that killing was a mark of respect. Benticles were just a really good laugh, with their little green feelings.

But these fellows, well. Darting and jumping like

stone-fleas, and not one with a decent thought you could bite into. And as for them psying us... now it gets really strange. As for psying us, they couldn't even see us. One crawled all over Auntie Zu, like she was some sort of food. The other kicked Xillu until she had to crumble. And poor old Mamod with his bouquet of rock-blossoms. They stood on his head, three of them, and communicated in squeaky chunks of air.

Once we'd got over the shock, we tuned in, slowed it all down, and this is what they said.

'Doesn't look good to me, Captain. I think we've made a miscalculation.'

'You're right, lieutenant. There's no sign of life on this planet. But the mineral resources look interesting.'

And they stayed two whole turns, and never so much as gave us the time of day. Mind you, several of us went home with them and I think it's done them some good.

Jackie Sullivan

Jackie Sullivan is an academic and former Head of Arts in a London community college; she bailed out without much of a safety net a year ago to enable her to excavate the artist within. A sometime professional artist and occasional writer, her focus during this year has been on the latter, specifically on what she regards as the interface between prose and poetry: micro-fiction. Several pieces have been published in Tears in the Fence during this time. Although impecunious, she has no regrets, feels fulfilled, and wishes she'd 'jumped' sooner; she blames the 60's.

Fading Faculties, Fainting Goats

I go down at dawn to make *tea,* the national bevy never touched before: it soothes, apparently. While the kettle boils I glimpse through the steam myself in a previous edition. I'm the Mommy, brown and brave in this curling photo; shoeless in Greece, rucksack on back, my little one Koala-style, in front. I wipe mist from the mirror and peer in. I don't see myself; *I'm* elsewhere, frozen in time, a week, five time zones, one pulling heart ago, still on the road in the U.S. of A.

I'd passed homeland security – *I do / do not bring: disease agents, cell-cultures, snails or soil;* we'd laughed or gasped from East to Mid-West, my Russian-doll baby / small child / magnificent grown woman, and I.

We drove, she in the driving seat, I with the map, through Atlantic pioneer towns of pastel-clad houses, where jewel-bright leaves drifted in tasteful amounts. We drank gin in log cabins where earth-smelling mountain towns, dampened by rapids, stream through the Catskills with film-set facades. On trails perpendicular we climbed to Bald Knob – with no little ribald remarking – as sunbeams pierced leaves of red, gold and lime like stained glass, and as summit mist lifted its veil like a flirt, for tantalising seconds, then closed in once more.

My navigating skills are not what they were. In the gloom we searched on, where mountains loomed over forests, for Robert Frost's birthplace – we'd taken the road less travelled too often. By moonlight Anna read from a hand-crafted sign, '*Fainting goats, and all kinds of gifts*'. I squinted helpfully. Farting goats? Needing neither, and still off course, we pressed on.

My girl turned thirty that month. Who was Mother in this rite of passage? Anna packed a powder-blue fleece to warm me, took the first bite of my apple to keep my bridge work from harm. We bought a seven dollar reflexology kit and I pummelled her feet in specified places – connected, it said, to the pelvis.

A lasting image of me and my daughter, on the forecourt of *Comfort:* we hugged crushing goodbyes – au revoirs! – and, as Moms are wont, I pointed to her feet… *now you know where your ovaries are, don't you, darling?*

Chloe Richards

Chloe Richards lives in a messy cottage with her partner and two young children and works as a marine biologist in Norfolk. She's currently working on a science fiction novel about a swarm of sentient plankton, using her job expertise to predict clever things about the future of submarining. She likes crisps and yoghurts a great deal, but wishes that she wasn't so inexplicably frightened of seaweed.

The Long Not Yet

You're not sure if the vicar doesn't sound like the microwave in your kitchen. He buzzes and bleeps about the altar, looking upset, and you're given to thinking they're actually paving slabs he's skipping between — a pavement full of cracks and uneven curbs. You watch his manic eyes and flailing robes and decide that *actually* he's the sort of man whose idea of parking on double-yellows is parking next to them, and because you find him compelling in precisely the way that he shouldn't be — like a man in a nightclub with sunglasses on — you giggle.

Inappropriately you think you hear his mother doing the same, though her noises are probably sobs you've only mistaken for a laugh, instead just something to accompany her hot wet cheeks and her twisted mouth, harsh lines at her eyes skewing off into her forehead.

You look at your feet, play with your cuticles.

There's another man now. It's his brother, slinking up to the microphone with a bowed head and a tensed back — the same one who fixes battleships in seedy docklands; the guy that your uncle teases about refurbishing the wars of our children. He talks as if he knew the body in the coffin, but you know better. It makes you scrunch your face up and rock your weight onto the other foot.

You look across at the body's wife, all clean teeth and smoky eyes and calf muscles; hips that sluice through a black dress, eyes that betray nothing. She looks only at his coffin, their two beautiful kids strapped to her legs with elegant sleeves and tailored mini-suits and no understanding whatsoever.

You look at the floor again — at all of the names carved

there. At all of the people beneath the pews beneath the concrete. Beneath your shoelaces and scuffed new shoes and awkwardly-lengthed skirt, and beyond the earshot of a man talking about his dead brother who he never really knew anyway.

And you feel absent – to these people, not from him – to these people in this church to whom you were only ever his childhood friend, barely even known as his teenage lover; the rest of the world having moved on so quickly from seventeen.

But your world has ended with the very same phone-call that told you his had.

Because at thirty you were still waiting.

Sara Browning

Sara Browning is going to be fifty this year and decided to mark the occasion by having fifty celebrations. To date she has had thirty one and having her story published in Leaf's anthology is certainly going to count for at least two more! She lives in the West Country with her husband, four dogs, two cats, a camper van with no engine called Priscilla and a caravan which is her writing sanctuary. She has two sons and a large extended family. Sara graduated from Bath Spa University in 2005 with a 2:1 in Creative Studies in English.

The Colour of Romance

'So are you trying to tell me that for fifty years people could only draw in eight different colours? That's a bit rubbish really.'

'Ah yes. But in 1949 things went really mad and another forty colours were added, so the world went from monochrome – well, octochrome maybe – to full-fat Technicolor.'

I was lying on the settee, a glass of wine precariously resting on my stomach and a tub of Pringles tucked between the cushions. My husband was, unadvisedly, questioning my knowledge of Crayola crayons.

'And what's more, there are now 120 colours to choose from, some having been replaced with lovely new ones, and some even being re-named. So what d'you think of that?'

'Well, yes. If you've got nothing better to do than spend an hour choosing between one shade of brown and another, that's fine.'

The conversation had started earlier when I'd announced I was writing a new story called 'The Demise of Prussian Blue' and Ray had said, in that distracted way he has when it comes to my writing, 'Russian who?'.

After I'd flounced off moaning that he never took me seriously, he'd eventually relented and asked where the title came from, which gave me just the opening I needed to develop the subject.

'Prussian Blue, introduced in 1949, changed its name to Midnight Blue in 1958 in response to teachers' requests.'

'That's probably because Prussia didn't exist anymore, or something. Or wasn't blue.'

'Apparently Prussian soldier's uniforms were blue. And Flesh was changed to Peach.'

'Very PC.'

'In 1958 they bought in sixteen more colours, including Indian Red which actually lasted until 1999 before they changed the name to Chestnut. Even more PC! And the biggest box had a built-in sharpener.'

Ray was lounging in his favourite chair, nursing a bottle of Stella and eyeing my Pringles. It's not often that we had time to sit and talk together; our lives were busy and full of other things. His job had become more and more demanding, causing him to lie awake at night twitching and sighing, and my novel, although only half written, had morphed into something quite unrecognisable. I lifted my head so I could see him more clearly. He was unusually quiet and had a far away look on his face.

He was definitely thinking.

I stretched and poked him questioningly with my toe. 'What?'

He looked at me and tipped his bottle in my direction.

'When I was little I got that box for Christmas. The one with the sharpener in it. My favourite colour was Raw Umber. I'd forgotten all about that. Raw Umber! Well I never. But I don't think it was the colour so much as the name. I drew on the kitchen wall and got a clip round the ear.'

'Awww! My all-time favourite was Burnt Sienna. It sounded so romantic.'

'Trust you!' He laughed; a deep, rich, golden sound that I realised had been absent for some time. I sat up.

'Do you want a Pringle?'

Varihi Scott

Varihi Scott was born in 1970 and currently lives in Scotland. She works in information and communications, moving back and forth between the private and voluntary sectors. The 2007 Leaf Books Micro-Fiction Competition is the first competition she has entered, and this is her first appearance in print.

Doing Something

I didn't take a homemade placard on the bus, so as not to give the impression that I was picketing the No.88 service. And I don't live near a fancy stationer, and Smiths weren't doing activists kits for beginners, and essentially, I don't like drawing that much attention to myself.

I scanned the tumult of plastic Argos sacks in the bags rack for signs of braver kindred spirits. There were none, or maybe the more experienced had special collapsible versions. I'd planned to attend the march with Claire but her mother had arrived with a suitcase and a list of grievances about Claire's father. The tear-muddled talks of sanctions, mediation, and counter-attack were embarrassing for a neutral to be around, so I left Claire doing her bit for world peace and set off to tackle the bigger picture on my own. My pulse quickened as the bus made a sluggish path through crawling vehicles caught in a diversion system caused by the march. How embarrassing to be late. I didn't fear being told I'd just missed an armistice agreement and should go home and wait for another war: it was that running to catch up with the tail end of the demonstration would look like such a lackadaisical commitment. The biographies of great social and political reformers never mention that the protagonist was a little delayed in her efforts due to being stuck in traffic.

The meeting point came into view and I breathed relief that my people hadn't left without me. The distant banners appeared to be sediment settling in a snow dome – disproportionately large blobs of white gently bouncing round the bottom of a miniature landmark. Bits of paper and card stapled to thin sticks, flimsy but held defiantly like oversized fly-swats: see your war? This is what we think of it. We swat it with the contempt it deserves. We don't storm parliament and swat the politicians… no, it's just — this is me. Here I am. My thoughts, in a pithy statement, printed on my office's computer. Then there are the bigger banners, the fabric ones held on poles and softly draping between two people. Some of them are improvised jobs painted on sheets: bed linen to your bombs! But most are beautiful collages of needlework and appliqué. Embroidery to your evil doings! Satin stitch to your war mongering! Patchwork to your deplorable plans! You put world leaders behind microphones to lie in deep authoritative voices; we're going to sing! Badly! You operate with men in uniform; we pull slogan t-shirts on over our jumpers, draw doves on our cheeks and stick stickers on our foreheads! Helmets? Ha! Face painting! It's love. What else could something so fragile and beautiful be, held up in the face of such power. And did we win? We are winning, and we found each other, so we can do more.

Louise McErlean

Louise D. McErlean lives in Belfast, Northern Ireland and is currently completing the final year of her Law & Spanish degree, following a year living in Zaragoza, Spain. She enjoys writing short stories and poetry in her spare time as well as salsa dancing. A nomadic instinct and love of new experiences have led her to travel to many places around the world, but most frequently to Edinburgh, known to friends as her home away from home.

The Silence of Sleeping with Him

Awakening beside him, the light barely escaping through the fine weave of the sun-patterned, tie-dyed sarong draped across the black and glass Edwardian window frames. Lying there listening to his breathing and watching, I notice he looks worried even in his sleep, but somehow animalistic, that instinctive sprawl of an animal satiated after carnal pleasure. But for now I let him lie. I consider taking a picture of his sleeping features with my phone, to later prove to myself that he was real and that this moment had indeed existed. I wonder if he ever had these silent moments observing as I did: did he ever wake in the night to look at me asleep under his arm and wonder if I was real? I doubt it. His breathing frightens me when he sleeps; at times his chest motionless, neither inhaling nor exhaling, then a gasp or a grunt and he takes a massive breath, reassuring me that I will not have to phone an ambulance. One that would arrive discovering the two of us naked together, wanting to contact her as next of kin.

Katy Whitehead

Katy Whitehead is a student on Warwick University's undergraduate creative writing course. She has previously received awards for writing, having entered competitions since the age of seven, as well as for acting and art. She is currently working on her first novel, *Purgatory*, about four girls' experiences interviewing at Oxford, at the fictional Purgatory College. She lives with several other creative writers whom she counts among her best friends and from whom she finds endless inspiration. Her hobbies include rock climbing, sarcasm and learning about the intricacies of the world, particularly the lie that is romantic love.

Unfortunate Noses

She was thirteen when she first had sex. The man was thirty-two and wore a straw hat, and they had gone to the yellow field behind the farm house with a plough-man's dinner of smiles of apple, cheese chunks and husks of bread, and after it was finished, she couldn't remember his name, or the colour of his hair, or anything except for the sky. Quite why she thought of this now, sitting opposite a man whose face she knew better than anyone's in the world, she wasn't sure. The age gap was similar but the situation couldn't be more different. Instead of hopping a fence and getting straight to it on the spread-out crumble of a muddy field, this was their seventh date, of sorts, with no more physical contact than a cheek kiss, the stroking of her palm with his index finger, the grazing of the fine down on her knee with his grown-up trousers. The menu that she held between two shaking fingers showed a three course meal a good deal more complex than the Cox and cheddar selection of that earlier occasion.

His sexual history read like a catalogue, and like buying from a catalogue he regretted most of the choices he had made, done so on image-basis alone. He always imagined that the appearance of a thing bore some steady correlation to its substance – that the way a girl dressed or gazed with big eyes across the room told something about her character, but each time this proved untrue. His favourite types were those with slightly unfortunate noses – too big, or crooked, or hooked: he saw a beauty that he imagined other men missed, and this made him feel that his attraction was personal, and that they would be grateful for it.

She had a perfect nose, in his eyes – meaning it was

grossly disproportionate to her face. It reminded him of his own. With her, the problem of unwrapping was irrelevant; he had seen her from every angle and knew not to expect surprises. She felt a sudden urgency to order, but what she wanted was not on the menu – a happily ever after, with this man, the white picket fence, all the things that would seem cliché to every other couple in the restaurant but that in this situation seemed burningly original, eccentric.

His love for her was genuine. Last night when he pulled the little linen blankets up to the chins of his children he felt a deep regret seep into every inch of his skin: if only they were hers. If only, and he could love them better. He had to scold himself under his breath for such a stupid wish: children as beautiful as that could never equate with this love of theirs. For one, they'd probably have six fingers, or learning difficulties. Isn't that what were always told is the end product of a love like this? Still, it'd be a pretty safe bet they'd have unfortunate noses.

Kate McAulay

Katy McAulay was born in 1981 and works as a copywriter for the University of Glasgow. She writes short stories, screenplays and recently completed her first novel, *White Friday*, while working towards a creative writing Masters. Her writing – creative, journalistic and otherwise – has appeared in newspapers, magazines, online and in the anthology *Outside of a Dog*. In her spare time, she plays, tours and learns with Mugenkyo taiko drummers. This keeps her mind from exploding and her muscles from sagging.

Floating is Easy

Actually, they called it euthanasia by omission, which means I didn't kill my mother, but it is true that I failed to raise the alarm one morning when I discovered that she had wandered out of my house during the night. It was this that my sister, who tried to have me convicted for her murder, objected to. This and the fact that instead of combing the traffic-filled streets for our missing relative, who had been suffering from Alzheimer's for three years, I chose to spend an hour in a flotation tank and the rest of the day as drunk as a teenager who has just had her first whiff of stolen vodka.

Floating was easy, only I wasn't sure what to do with my hands. Leaving them to float by my sides made me feel exposed. More naked somehow. I had fold to them over my stomach. I felt a burning sensation between my legs as the water entered me. Then… nothing. As the light in the tank shrank I thought about the people busily tramping the pavements outside. They had no idea that I was in there, alone and silent and drifting.

Maybe this is what it feels like to be dead.
Shutupshutupshutup.

My mother they found curled up and cold in the classroom of the school where she used to teach before her brain unravelled sufficiently to cause them to relieve her of her post. Caring woman that she was, she had fed and watered class 4A's guinea pig before she died.

When they happened, the court proceedings weren't nearly as exciting as I thought they would be, except the lawyer husband of the only friend who had stuck by me persuaded the authorities not only to pronounce me innocent of the charge, but to pay me a significant amount of money due to the fact that technically, *technically*, my mother died due to blood loss from a head injury she sustained from a fall in the premises of the school. Apparently, a cleaner had left a damp sponge on the floor.

When it was all done, I tried to sign over the majority of my acquired funds to one of those crestfallen graduates that adorn so many street corners nowadays, selling charity direct debits and occasionally wondering what the hell they're doing. It's kind of funny if you think about it, because up until that point I had always slalomed around anyone wearing an Oxfam t-shirt with my eyes to the pavement, just like everyone else.

After a confused twenty minutes he informed me that the most he could do to help was to accept a maximum direct debit payment of £50 a month from me, and sign me up for an Inca Trail hike for a minimum deposit of £300 that I would then earn back by collecting sponsorship.

This is a strange and a cruel world and no mistake.

Nancy Saunders

Nancy Saunders is many things: being a writer plays a regretfully small part. She is also a mother, an other-half, a fiddle-player, a Francophile, a library assistant, a dreamer, an inhabitant of Bristol and a terribly remiss member of Alex Keegan's Boot Camp. When Nancy *has* knuckled down to writing she has won a couple of competitions and been honourably mentioned in a handful of others.

When my third foot grows

When my third foot grows I will call it Bob, or Nelson, or perhaps something good and kind, like Miranda. Maybe then my foot will be safe from getting lost. I was very careless, see, with that second one. I should have treated it better, taken more notice. Then maybe I wouldn't have a piece of me missing.

I've got to be ready; ready for whatever comes next. Don't let on to anyone, but I felt the beginnings of something late last night. I was half watching the weatherman promise sun for tomorrow, and half listening to the rain throw arrows at the window, when it happened. Just a tingle at first, a tiny electric wave brushing across my skin. Then much bigger, like hundreds of pins and needles tumbling towards that great lummox of a foot-shaped hole. I sat up, grabbed hold of the torch I keep by me for emergencies, and pulled my leg up to get a closer look. There, right where my ankle used to be, something knobbly was pushing its way out, real slow and gentle, like, but there. No mistake about it: my third foot was on its way. I let out an almighty whoop, hopped over the settee and three times round the coffee table. I made enough of a racket to wake the dead and, sure enough, Mrs McDermott screeched from downstairs, punching holes in her ceiling with Hail Marys and a broom handle. I retaliated with a few more rounds of the room and several 'shut-up you stupid old lady's.

So, you see, it won't be long now. If a foot's anything like a bud, or a leaf, I'll be waving my third foot around in no time.

Miranda. Miranda used to laugh and say, 'If you really love me, you'll love my toes.' And I did. I do. Every last one of them. And then it happened. Miranda took on enough work for the two of us. She'd come home from the shop, smile – all done in – shoulders hanging, but not a complaint out of her. I'd say, 'Sit down, love, take the weight off.' I'd undo her shoes, peel her socks off real carefully, and squeeze away the day from her feet. I was trying to balance things out, see. Somehow. I wanted to look after Miranda. It's the toes that I miss. One lot of little piggies in the bed just don't seem to be enough.

There we go: definite movement from the ankle. I've measured two inches since this morning, and there's all these sticky out bits, like branches almost, pushing down underneath my skin. These must be the new bones, after which will come the branches of the foot, and then, my all-new row of toes.

Stupid bugger. Can't stop myself from crying. This time tomorrow I will be a whole person again. I won't go to sleep. I want to be here when Miranda comes.

David Hallett

David Hallett was born in the East-End of London in 1965 and has lived most of his adult life abroad. He is currently living in France at the foot of the Jura mountains. He runs a website design company and has spent his working life so far as a graphic designer and IT consultant. A keen but unskilled musician and an only slightly better singer/songwriter, he has recently turned his attention to fiction. He wishes there were more hours in the day.

Bridged Perspective

The bridges were laid out below me, straight and true, crossing each other at equal intervals and stretching off in all directions like a lesson in perspective.

I wondered what the bridges connected. It was hard to see from up here. The first time I noticed them it seemed like they didn't really connect anything at all.

But now I could see small shapes, slightly darker shadows, clustered along the bridges themselves.

So, in-between the bridges could be water. I hadn't spotted that before.

I bent over to try and get a better look. Yes, it was starting to make sense. All this time I had thought the spaces in between the bridges were land, but now I realised: the bridges ran over water, and the dark shapes were the land.

Not for the first time a very small boat worked it's way slowly into view, oars pumping away furiously on both sides.

I casually moved my foot and gently squashed the boat.

Some of the oars still moved. I thought I could even see the tiller-man struggling for control of his stricken craft, wriggling and writhing at the stern. Or perhaps I imagined that. It was so small how could I possibly have seen that? C'mon, stay rational. This is exciting, and new. The bridges run over water. File it away under 'fact'.

I reached forwards and pulled hard. There was violent spinning, a flamboyant display.

I always pull too hard. And it ends up soggy and useless because it lands on the floor. And there's never enough even though you seem to spend half your life getting more.

I noticed the oars had stopped moving now, all bar one, still making the occasional gesture of defiance. I squashed the boat again, hard this time. It looked like a very small splodge of jam.

Now the space around me was starting to shrink. Do you remember? I told you before. Spaces shrink and grow.

I stood up and looked down at the bridges, which were worrying me as usual. If you go near the bridges they will get you. Stay away from the bridges. If you ever go there, I mean. It's not all bridges; it's just these bridges. Your bridges are probably okay.

I hope.

You should check first, actually. Just to be sure.

I reached down and started to get myself straight. I used to call for help with that, but she taught me how and I can do it on my own now. Then I opened the door and tip-toed out, being careful not to go near the bridges.

Just as my feet inched to safety I reached back in and pulled the chain.

Laurie Porter

Laurie Porter decided at age seven that she would be an artist and writer when she grew up and has been a little bit of both over the years alongside her many other jobs (the strangest of which involved monitoring mould growth on bread). She has been published on paper three times, online a couple of times, and has been frustratingly short-listed more times than that. She lives in the UK with a bunch of amazing people and some animals. In a good week she'll manage to write something, anything.

We'll Meet Again

It's that time again. Henry gets in from the post office, having collected his pension, and is making a cup of tea when he sees the light flashing on his answerphone. He knows it's Arthur. It's always Arthur.

Henry won't bother to listen to the message until he's finished his tea and done the crossword. In fact, he might not bother to listen at all. He's fed up with all this. But he knows that if he ignores it, Arthur will just ring again, and again, and again. He could unplug the phone, he supposes – Arthur is the only one who ever rings – but what if he missed that important call from Edna's daughter? The call that will end all this?

'Henry,' the message goes, 'it's Arthur.' Arthur tells him there's a fresh one dug at St Stephen's – scheduled for filling at noon tomorrow. Meet him there at 8.30 tonight unless he hears otherwise. Henry starts to dial Arthur's number to tell him he won't be there, but he knows he has no option. It's a debt he's been paying off for years – one he'll be paying until that call comes. Sleep with your best friend's girl and you pay for it for the rest of your life. One night in '45, that was all. One night that changed everything. One night that saw Arthur and Edna going their separate ways forever.

Henry is first to arrive. It's a dark night. He wanders among the gravestones, running his hands over the worn names so familiar now. He hears Arthur's footsteps. The two shake hands. Henry says he hopes Arthur's well and Arthur says he's fed up with all this. Arthur berates Henry for sounding so solemn. They make their way to plot 292B. Arthur gets out his tape measure and Henry holds the torch and helps him. It's the right size. It usually is but Arthur likes to measure anyhow. Arthur tells Henry he thinks it's a good plot; by daylight it will lie in the shade of the oak. Henry agrees. Arthur stoops to lift off the plastic and Henry makes a cursory attempt to help him. The graveyard is eerily quiet tonight in the absence of a full moon. Henry knows Arthur is wearing his best suit. It'll get muddy as he lowers himself down into the freshly dug hole. It takes Arthur a lot longer to get in and out these days. Twenty years ago it wasn't so bad, but you know... with the arthritis. Henry settles himself down on a tilted headstone to keep watch, takes out his flask and pours himself a coffee.

Arthur settles down for the night in the grave. He does this in case. He lies there all night just in case tomorrow it will be Edna's. He lies there so he can say that for one night, just one night, he, like Henry, slept in the same place as Edna.

Michael Massey

Michael Massey teaches in a rural primary school in Co.Kilkenny, Ireland where he also co-ordinates the Clogh Writers Group. He is primarily a poet and has published two poetry collections. He is currently working on a third collection.

Sailing to Valhalla

The bar of the lakeside hotel belched out its last two customers of the night. They sit now in a long boat sheltered by the curved arm of the pier, organising themselves and their thoughts before they do what they have to do. The younger man stares at where the moon should be.

'Hey, Charlie, d'ya think this old tub of Eric's'll get us over and back?'

'Don't fret, Tony m'boy, it's as safe as a house on fire.'

'Bad image, Charlie.'

'No. No. Good image. Eric'll be goin' in a blaze of glory.'

With these words a silence descends. It engulfs them like a fog. You could slice it with a sharp knife. They stare into the darkness. At last Charlie turns to his younger friend.

'Taught us everything we know 'bout boats, did Eric. And a lot more.'

'Amen,' says Tony.

Charlie eases the long boat out into the calm waters of Lough Ree, rowing with a smooth, easy rhythm, hardly breaking the water's skin.

'Did ya know this is the centre of Ireland? The bloody dead centre,' says Charlie.

Tony does not see any need to answer. Again they lapse into heavy silence.

The moon sails out from behind a cloud. The two men pull the boat up the shingle beach of the small island. They approach a tent, silhouetted. They stoop in, re-emerge minutes later lugging a stiff sleeping bag between them.

Laboured breathing, rhythmic lap of lake water and shingle crunching underfoot are the only sounds in the night. They lay their burden in the long boat, then turn to dismantle the tent.

Later, on the mainland, they stand on the pier looking out over the water. In the moonlight they see the long boat drifting towards the centre of the lake. Aboard is the lumpy sleeping bag, in flames. A white wispy rope of smoke spirals back towards them. Their eyes smart. Charlie wraps his long arms 'round the outboard engine, turns, hauls it to the car. Tony follows.

Caroline Adams

Caroline Adams is a creative writing tutor with the Open University and a novelist. Her first novel *Taking Something Small* is resting at the moment with Annette Green Authors' Agency. She has written numerous short stories all of whom are looking for good homes and some troublesome poems who are frequently to be found under the arches on the Brighton seafront, drunk and disorderly and served with ASBOs.

Car Park

We met in a car park. 'Trust me,' you said. 'Everything will be simple. You drive in and park. Get out. Pop the trunk like you're gonna take something out. Then look at your watch. Seem to change your mind. And close the trunk again.'

I did as you said. I'd have done anything for you back then. Anything.

We worked the clubs for a year. I met the boys coming off the ferry at Dover. Conversation was polite and to-the-point, always with a bottle of duty-free scotch thrown in. A handshake later and I kicked down hard on the automatic pedal of our borrowed Audi Quattro Convertible and ripped up the coast road, stopping only for chocolate and chips.

At the multi-story car-park next to the cinema multiplex, which was showing on multiple-screens all nine sequels of the action flick you favoured, I drove to the eighth floor, and parked in a numbered bay – a multiple of the date in the month.

'Never talk to Roger,' you said. Your eyes were black as liquorice. Your skin like bleached paper. 'Keep it neat. Keep it small. That's my motto.'

Last night you didn't show though. Bats nesting in the concrete girders overhead flitted out at dusk. Rows of liverish strip-lights hummed into life. Voices from the street mixed with metallic thuds, screeching tyres and the cough of exhausts.

I remembered how we met. I was lost and needed directions to the Lido. You were the third person I asked that day. You walked me there. We talked all the way. It took five hours. I was fourteen and hungry. I'd been living on packets of M&Ms for days. Over the years I came to know you. I could always find you at that stall on the seafront, selling plastic sunglasses with designer logos and photographs of burning buildings. I thought you were waiting until I was old enough but my birthday came and went and that was not it. That was not what you were after.

Last night, in the car park, it grew cold and still you did not come. The goods settled in their polythene bags. The reek of petrol stung my throat. I had your rival's number on speed dial. Someone with a name like Roger. I remembered what you told me. So I called him.

While I waited it grew colder and at one point I squatted beside the bonnet of my borrowed Peugeot 206 Cabriolet. A stream of warm piss ran between my sandaled feet, spreading out in a golden lake beneath the chassis.

'Never trust anyone over nineteen,' you once said. 'I never have and it works for me every time.'

I turned twenty that week.

Betrayal is a fat manila envelope through a rolled down window. Cigar smoke to mask the tang of urine. 'Never talk to Roger,' a voice from inside said. His jag purred as it pulled away. The walls echoed car engine noise back at me like applause.

Matthew Mead

Matthew Mead is a second year Philosophy undergrad at Cambridge University, although he originally came to read Music. When not in Cambridge, he lives in the countryside near Worcester.

Cl$_2$

Mr Gratland had retired once, but now he was back. Having spent twenty years teaching and saving enough money to do things, he found he had not had the time to develop interests. Prior to teaching he had been a chemist, mixing large batches of chemicals every day. Sometimes he had used hydrofluoric acid, which soaks through the skin and burns the flesh before the nerves feel it. The children liked this detail, but other anecdotes from those years left them nonplussed. Slowly, only this one attention-grabbing snippet was recalled, the others dispensed with. Instead he would talk about Mrs Gratland. Apparently Mrs Gratland would not let him go to the pub even though the maths teachers invited him. The children smirked.

This morning he was involved in an incident. A boy was trying to leave class and he had caught him in the hall. The boy had thrust his chest out and stepped up close. Mr Gratland called out to a nearby teaching assistant who was sat at a desk. He asked her to act as a witness, calling out each move the boy made. Then he tried to push the boy away a little, but he protested loudly:

'Why are you pushing me? You can't do that.' The voice had the confident lilt you hear before a fight. The boy stepped closer. Mr Gratland called again to the witness. She sat with an amused looked on her face. Then Mr Smith, head of RS came out. He was taller than the boy, who was taller than Mr Gratland. The child was dealt with and Mr Gratland left. The witness remained seated.

Now it was the fourth lesson of the day. The lab technician had readied the chemicals for the experiment and retreated to the store. It was a nice day, but all the windows were closed. In came Year 11. Mr Gratland asked them to leave again and come in quietly. They did so, but he left them standing for a while anyway. Someone had changed a name on the register as a joke. It was read out. The boy turned red. The girls laughed. They went over the theory for today's reaction, and the class sat through some jokes about Mr Gratland's home life.

It was a simple reaction: $NaOCl + HCl > NaCl + H_2O + Cl_2$. Bleach and acid produce a salt, water and chlorine gas. The only apparatus needed was a beaker, a test tube and a test tube rack.

Everyone had the bleach in the test tube. Mr Gratland gave the order to add the acid. The reaction began and after a while a greenish tinge could be seen through the glass. He told the children to smell it to confirm it was chlorine. They stuck their noses up close and breathed in. Some of them coughed a little. Mr Gratland stood at the front of the class watching them see who had the tube that would make them reel the most.

Amy Sackville

Amy Sackville was educated at Leeds and Oxford and now lives in West London, where she is currently working on her first novel. She came second in Fish Publishing's short story competition in 2006 with 'Beach', and has previously had reviews and articles published in various magazines, journals and papers. She is interested in the way that identities are built out of language, and its fracture and failure.

Signalling

Sandra stares at the road ahead, determinedly speechless, feeling lightheaded and tired and irritable. Beside her Richard drives with just one finger on the wheel as if to annoy her on purpose. Occasionally clicking his tongue against his teeth, barely audible. Wishing he was home with a beer, in front of the TV, not stuck here watching line after line swallowed up by the bonnet. He's going to miss the news now. Wanted to leave earlier but couldn't drag her away, sick of an afternoon with tipsy aunts and leering uncles and trying not to stare at Sandra's cousin, who is far too provocative to be convincingly seventeen. He knows his driving is lazy and a little too fast. He veers out to overtake and can hear Sandra not saying anything. Steals a glance and sees the little pucker at the corner of her mouth. Her lipstick's rubbed off on all those champagne glasses that her mother will be washing in the morning to take back to the supermarket. And Roberta and James will be in their hotel room already, she'll be squeaking away by now no doubt, the first of a life's nights of tedious conjugal bliss. Those hips of hers are worryingly child-bearing. He is not feeling very avuncular. Clicks his tongue against his teeth.

Checking the rearview he sees Jack gazing, needy, at his mother. There's raspberry coulis crusting on his cheek. Christ.

Jack is considering, carefully, if there is something he might do that would make them all laugh, that would make them pleased with him, that his father won't call showing off. He flushes again at the memory of being told to settle down, in front of his uncle, his cousins. He shifts uncomfortably under his father's glance. Before getting into the car they tried to persuade him to take off his tie, jacket and waistcoat, and now, having refused, he must keep them on all the way home. Sweaty, hot, itchy, and tight. He can feel his belly pushing against the buttons. He ate a lot of something called Coronation Chicken, and potato salad, and profiteroles and two helpings of pavlova, and everyone said what a little gentleman he was and his uncle gave him a glass of champagne. And now he thinks he might like to be sick or go to the toilet but the silence has lasted so long and he doesn't want to ask.

He looks out of the window. Close by, he counts seven cranes, black against the deep sky, the sky almost violet, almost orange, almost black but the cranes are blacker, their red lights blinking at the tips. Tall and identical and impossibly high, impossibly far above them.

'Look, Jack, cranes', says Sandra, the sudden sound of her own voice surprising her, before she turns to see that her son is already gazing at them, eyes wide and shining. He doesn't hear her; he is terrified, but he doesn't cry.

Alice Blake

Alice Blake has been writing for many years now. She has seven
grandchildren with whom she plays and whom she hugs and kisses
frequently. She lives with her husband on the shores of a golden
lake and spends her days talking to her friends, writing, painting,
singing with her band, swimming in the summer, skiing in the
winter and making love to her gorgeous man all year round. She
is a writer of fiction.

Looking Down

Fairly spectacular, isn't it? Reminds me of that time we went up the Post Office tower when we were boys. Remember? I'm glad you didn't have to do all that queuing for the lifts tonight though… or should I say standing in line for the elevators? You'd really not have enjoyed that; I can just imagine your impatience, jiggling your leg and looking at the ceiling. I didn't mind… just standing, watching the other people. But we were always different like that, weren't we? Still, we're here now. Just look. Fantastic eh? Fuck, this is great. Come on; let's walk all the way round.

Bit of a freezing wind though, isn't it? Wish I'd brought a scarf. Remember that Doctor Who scarf your girlfriend knitted you. Ha, that nearly killed me, getting caught under the wheels of that taxi. Dunno why I had it that time. It didn't survive. I nearly didn't survive.

I guess you're not really feeling the cold. Lucky bastard. Or not.

So, how's Mum? Okay? Yeah, Dad's okay; saw him last week. Still in the hospital but they said he was stable. Well, I wouldn't be here if he wasn't, would I? Yeah, still moaning about this and that and the state of the world. Misses you and Mum. Always does. I don't think he'll be seeing you just yet though. Well… hope not anyway.

Look – I reckon that's the Statue of Liberty. Bit small to make out though. Hang on; let's use one of these binocular things. Yes, look, that's her. Coming there tomorrow with me? Great.

Well, I think we've seen all there is to see tonight. And I'm freezing my balls off here. Yeah, don't bother with the gift shop, I'll get some mementos for the kids. Shame they're not here too. Mine and yours. With their Mums. At least they have mum's, eh? Not like us. But we had each other, didn't we?

Ok, right. Bye. Tomorrow on Ellis Island then? Bye.

Arvon P Whitaker

Arvon P Whitaker doesn't believe you'd be terribly interested in his biography.

This is his first publication.

Morris came in from the garden shed

Morris came in from the garden shed and tossed the pliers onto the draining board. They landed in a lidless Bavarian tankard, half-full of something wet and potent. The clangs and splashes made the boys glance up from the crown green bowling.

'Were the pliers not the thing?' asked Gordon.

'Not subtle enough,' said Morris. 'It's tweezers I need, but I've not seen mine in months. They were good tweezers too. I won them in a luxury Christmas cracker.'

'It's a fair bet,' said Rupert, 'that Kelvin has your tweezers. He'd lift a tub of ceramic baking beans or a wooden-handled steak knife or a beaten tin slide-whistle if you forgot to tie it down.'

'I thought so too,' said Morris. 'But Kelvin says not.' And he picked up the corkscrew and carried it thoughtfully to the shed.

Rupert played with the volume.

'What do you fancy he wants with the tweezers that he can do just as well with a corkscrew?' asked Gordon.

'It'll be a plucking thing,' said Rupert. 'Or a splinter in the pad of his finger.'

'It's a beast of a splinter that needs a corkscrew to get it out,' said Gordon.

Morris came in with the sledgehammer over his shoulder and looked sweatily about the kitchen. Gordon propped an arm on the back of the sofa.

'Is Kelvin helping you in the shed then?' he asked.

'He is,' said Morris, and looked at the tankard. 'Is that meths?'

'You're thinking that because it took the rust off the pliers,' said Rupert, noting Morris' falling face. 'But I believe it's only vodka.'

'Was the corkscrew useful?' asked Gordon.

'It was more useful than the pliers,' said Morris, and headed off again with a box of very sharp needles.

'Do you think...?' said Rupert.

'Well,' whispered Gordon, 'if he *has* packed Kelvin full of splinters – and he's looking for the tweezers – at least that shows a modicum of remorse on his part and a desire not to bestow anything in the way of permanent harm on Kelvin.'

Rupert frowned. 'Perhaps he's bent on removing things that were already present in Kelvin and are somehow integral to his essential well-being.'

'Like eyebrows, you mean? And toenails and nasal hair?'

'And *tonsils*, I was thinking. And the *lashes* of his eyes and possibly even his septum.'

'And could you not remove a kidney from a man with a well-honed set of tweezers if you had in you the required degree of animosity and a good strong stomach and lots of surgical alcohol?'

Morris breezed in and swept up a fish-slice. He paused in the doorway.

'I'll get my tweezers,' he said, and was gone.

'If Kelvin gives my eggcup back,' said Rupert, 'I think I won't feel so bad about myself.'

'If Morris finds a way to mangle us with an eggcup,' said Gordon, 'I'm giving Kelvin all I own tied up with a silver ribbon.'

They nodded and looked pointedly at the Bowls.

Shaun Manning

Shaun Manning has written for print, web, stage, and radio. His work has been featured on BBC Radio 4 and Second City's Skybox Theatre in Chicago. Shaun has also served as editor on an annual comic book anthology and the online journal FromGlasgowToSaturn.co.uk. Shaun is currently working on his first novel, *Pizza Good Times*. When not in Glasgow, Shaun lives mostly in the midwestern United States.

Queen of the Nerd Prom

Every year, I look forward to it. It's the one place I can dress up and be beautiful, where for just a little while I've got everybody's eyes on me. And every year, I'm reminded why, each time, I come away depressed. The comic book convention never fails to disappoint.

I spend weeks on my costume, just like every year, and wake up early on Friday morning to prepare. I'm not kidding myself: I'm no beauty when it comes to going about every day, tramping down to school, working part time at the Pizza Hut. But in my costume, each year when I dress up, I look good. And this year, I look super hot, but I knew that already, when I was thinking up my character, when I assembled the material for my outfit. And the boys notice me, like I wanted. But not like I wanted. It's always some greasy thirty-year old guy in a Green Lantern t-shirt (classic or modern, doesn't matter) asks me if I'm painted blue 'all over'. Well, it would be silly to spend hours painting ninety-some percent of my body and leave the rest all pinky, wouldn't it? It's a little bit messy, and I can't really sit down without ruining everything, but you just have to make sure the paint sets, you know, before you put on the shorts and top. But this answer would only wind him up, and anyway He's Not the Droid I'm Looking For. So I give him a nasty look and push on. The boys my own age give me a look of a different sort, but they're either too shy to approach or more concerned with impressing their friends by quoting Kevin Smith dialogue to comment on my appearance.

Pulled aside for some photos, I get to strike a pose and

everything seems all right. I've been practising, and I've got the posture just right. Sometimes there's another 'costume' in the picture, a passing Lex Luthor or Spider-man or Captain Jack Sparrow. Captain Sparrow is a new addition. I'm really starting to hate pirates. Not as much as I hate Cosplay Girls (freaking animé poseurs), but still, these guys put on some eye shadow and think they're Johnny Depp. Gag me. Sometimes it's another girl in the picture with me. Sometimes the photographer asks us to kiss. I don't like to think about the pictures after they're taken.

The year I was born, the Joker shot Batgirl through the spine. Comic fans are still crying about the sexism of it all, that she's still crippled in a world where any injury can be healed by magic. Next year, I'm dressing as her.

Robin Tompkins

Robin Tompkins was a cat in a previous life and hopes to be one again someday. He has been telling stories all his life like his father before him and writing them down for nearly as long. He is a self-taught writer who discovered on the eve of his fiftieth birthday that he was to be published for the very first time. Robin Tompkins is celebrating still.

Fading Footprints

They are almost gone now, almost level with the surrounding snow. You would hardly know they were there, but I know. A line of footprints: arrow straight, the length of my long garden path, disappearing into the gnarled, old yews bowed down with the soft weight of snow.

It has been a longstanding dream of mine, to buy a little place in the Cotswolds, retire and watch the seasons change. I did, I have and the pleasure it gives me is immense.

It will come as no surprise to you, then, if I say that I spent yesterday evening, drink in hand in the firelight, staring out of the darkened window at winter's first snowfall, snowflakes flurrying out of a huge silvery moon like white bats from a cave mouth.

That's how I know I didn't make the footprints, you see: the snow started after I got home and yet there they were this morning, well-defined in the crisp, sparkling snow.

What's so odd about that? The paperboy, or the milkman, you say? I have neither delivered. It's one of my little pleasures to walk down the lane to the village in whatever weather I'm sent to fetch them. The postman? No. There was nothing in the hall this morning, and besides – and this is the really odd bit – the footprints lead up to my door, but none lead away. The village children then, teasing the newcomer? Well, perhaps… but I don't think so. Let me explain.

Obeying a curious certainty, I went to the French windows at the rear. It's a nice aspect: a long lawn sweeps down to the river, flanked by topiaries like giant chess pieces. I can take no credit for them; they came with the house.

There were the footprints again, leading away from the house in an unbroken line, crossing the river to emerge on the far bank, marching on until they were lost in the pinkish snow light and the blue-grey horizon. As I watched, the snow began to fall again: huge flakes, soft as feathers, fluffing and plumping the landscape.

I was in my dressing-gown, yet I felt compelled to go out and examine the prints before the fresh snow buried them. The air had a pearly brightness and a take-your-breath-away freshness. The little trident-shaped tracks of hopping birds crossed the prints and the track of something else, a cat or a fox probably, trailed them for a little way. Feeling the cold, I crunched back into the house through pure white snow, my slippers sodden. It was then that it occurred to me. I took a roll of paper towels from the kitchen and unravelled them across the living room carpet, tamping them down gently as I did so. Sure enough, there they were: long, wet patches evenly spaced.

Jane Rusbridge

Jane Rusbridge has an MA in Creative Writing from Chichester University, where she is an associate lecturer teaching at both undergraduate and postgraduate levels. She writes in a shed at the bottom of the garden. Her stories have won or been placed in several competitions, including the Fish Prize (2006), the Bridport Prize (2003, 2006) and the Writersinc Writer-of-the-year award (2005), and stories and poems have also been published in various magazines and anthologies such as *The Interpreter's House* and *Mslexia* (2006). Her first novel, *The Devil's Music,* has just been taken on by an agent. Jane is married to a farmer and lives by the sea in West Sussex.

The Corn Carter

You are big and blond and block the light from the
window. Behind me are empty rooms but I smile, hand
over paintbrush, roller, a tin of paint. Your few words shoot
staccato, Gestapo consonants cutting the air.

All morning it rains and, in another room, I hear boots
on bare boards, the scrape of a stool. But later you carry
your cup to the kitchen to soak in the sink and I realise
you're young enough to be my son. Suddenly you speak.
Slow, steady, as if you have not spoken for a long time but
now you can, and you tell me how much you love corn-
carting after the winter in London, how you sit on the
tractor, look across flat miles to the Downs and remember
the sky and rocks that fill the open red distances of the
Karoo.

You dislike our square green lawns and straight fences.

You mention your mother. Once a week she drives to
the nearest village, waits for you to telephone the General
Store.

You are learning German, because it is beautiful and
sounds like Afrikaans.

And as you talk, I wonder about living with bars on
windows, guns on bedside tables, fearful of a magic you say
blecks can work on even the most ferocious guard dog.

All through supper the children wriggle and laugh
behind their hands at your name.

Only a few weeks later, they chase you around the garden
calling, *Norman! Norman!* begging you to return with them
to the pool, where you propel the smooth water into a
turmoil of waves simply by walking round and round, faster
and faster.